For Emily, who walked the whole way with me
J. D.

For Julia, a friend of the heart
E. B. G.

Text copyright © 2017 by Julia Denos
Illustrations copyright © 2017 by E. B. Goodale

First edition 2017

Library of Congress Catalog Card Number pending
ISBN 978-0-7636-9035-9

17 18 19 20 21 22 APS 10 9 8 7 6 5 4 3 2

Printed in Humen, Dongguan, China

This book was typeset in Berling.
The illustrations were done in ink, watercolor, letterpress, and digital collage.

Candlewick Press
99 Dover Street
Somerville, Massachusetts 02144

visit us at www.candlewick.com

WINDOWS

Julia Denos

illustrated by E. B. Goodale

Candlewick Press

At the end of the day, before the town goes to sleep,
you can look out your window . . .

and see more little windows
lit up like eyes in the dusk,

blinking awake as the lights turn on inside:
a neighborhood of paper lanterns.

You can take a walk, out your door
into the almost-night.

You might pass a cat

or an early raccoon

taking a bath
in squares of yellow light.

One window might be tall,
with the curtains drawn,

or small,
with a party inside.

Between two windows,
there could be a phone,
used for good ideas.

There might be a hug,

 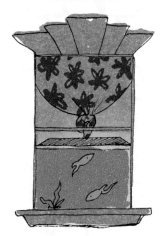 

or a piano,

and someone might be learning to dance.

Another window could be dark,
with a sleeping plant or two,

or maybe bright and rounded,
like the moon.

Some windows will have dinner, or TV.

Others are empty
and leave you to fill them up
with stories.

Then you arrive home again,
and you look at your window from the outside.
Someone you love is waving at you,

and you can't wait to go in.

So you do.